WHO IS THE
SOCK FAIRY?

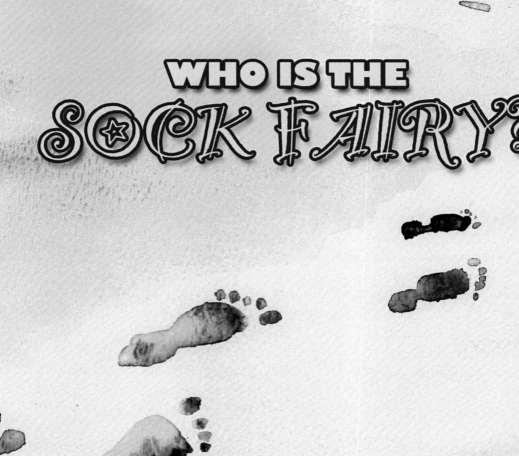

STORY BY
HOLLY
DANOWSKI

ILLUSTRATIONS BY
CHRIS
DOUGLAS

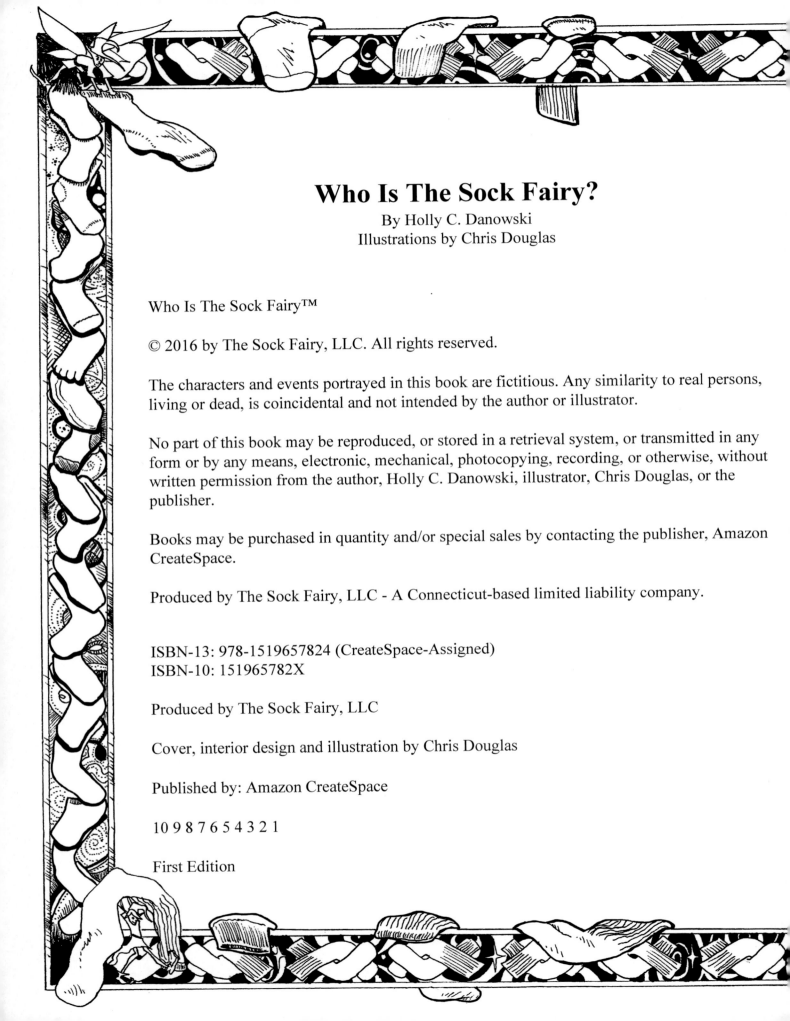

Who Is The Sock Fairy?

By Holly C. Danowski
Illustrations by Chris Douglas

Books may be purchased in quantity and/or special sales by contacting the publisher, Amazon CreateSpace.

Produced by The Sock Fairy, LLC - A Connecticut-based limited liability company.

ISBN-13: 978-1519657824 (CreateSpace-Assigned)
ISBN-10: 151965782X

Produced by The Sock Fairy, LLC

Cover, interior design and illustration by Chris Douglas

Published by: Amazon CreateSpace

10 9 8 7 6 5 4 3 2 1

First Edition

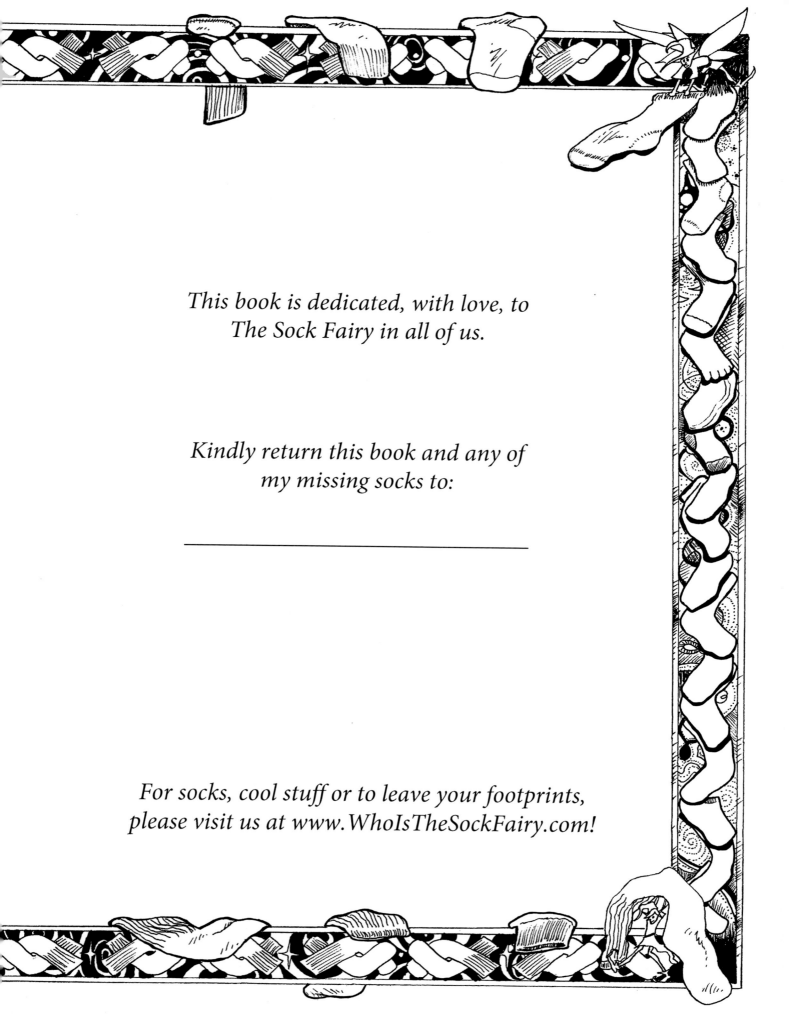

This book is dedicated, with love, to
The Sock Fairy in all of us.

Kindly return this book and any of
my missing socks to:

_____

For socks, cool stuff or to leave your footprints,
please visit us at www.WhoIsTheSockFairy.com!

My feet felt like ice cubes
When I crawled into bed.
But when the sun woke me up
They were toasty instead.

And both my socks were back on.
My feet were no longer bare.
Somebody noticed.
Somebody cared!

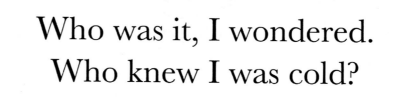

Who was it, I wondered.
Who knew I was cold?

I have so many questions
Here's what I was told.

But, who is The Sock Fairy?
When does she come?
What does she look like?
Where is she from?

Does she get as excited as I
When my feet grow and grow?
Will she be the one who discovers
That my toe made a hole?

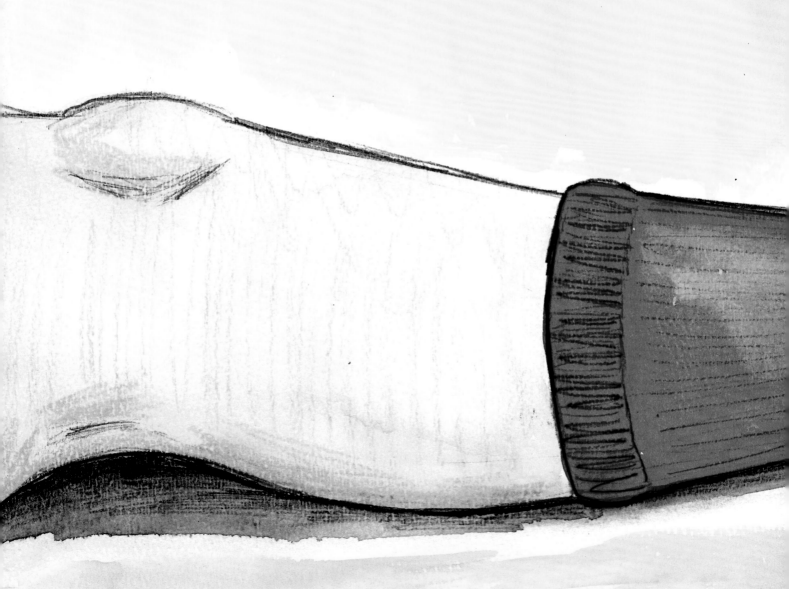

Oh, she thinks it's fantastic!
Bringing you socks is her goal
"Eureka!" she says,
As she measures the hole!

The Sock Fairy will do it!
This is how she has fun!
Socks for you, Socks for me!

Socks for E-v-e-r-y ONE!

But how does she know
When my ten toes are cold?
And does she bring new socks
When my favorites get old?

What if my socks become stinky,
Will that catch her off guard?
What if I play without shoes on
Outside in the yard?

Does she track where socks go
When one loses its twin?
Does she know what to do
When the heels wear thin?

Does she look in the washer
In case one clings to the side?
Does she know whose is whose
Once the socks are all dried?

Oh, she DOES, yes, she does!
She checks each one with care.
Matching sizes and colors,
Sorting them all into pairs.

The Sock Fairy gets it!
She juggles socks by the ton!
Socks for you, socks for me!

Socks For E-v-e-r-y One!

But WHO is The Sock Fairy?
WHEN does she come?
WHAT does she look like?
WHERE does she come from?

That is such a great question!
Where DOES she come from?
It must be a place, oh so wondrous,
A Sock Fairy Kingdom?!

Some socks are quite fuzzy
With brilliant, bright hues,
Add some sparkles and rainbows,
For parties right in your shoes.

Spiders, footballs or peace signs,
Shamrocks, kittens and bows,
Smiling Pumpkins or Penguins
When colder wind blows.

You can play dress up with argyles,
You might choose white ones with lace.
Or colored stripes on your sports socks
When you put on your "Game Face".

The Sock Fairy won't accept money
How it works is quite neat.
She gets paid by the footprints
You leave with YOUR FEET!

The Sock Fairy is happy to help you.
Always knowing just what to do.
Did you know that with or without socks,
Your FEET know it too?

Try balancing on one foot,
Using only one of your feet.
You can even dance barefoot
Moving both feet to the beat!

The Sock Fairy knows this SO WELL.
She's your feet's biggest fan!
She lovingly helps you
Stand STRONG where you stand.

But she also knows this
A busy day lies ahead.
It's time to take off your socks
And get ready for bed.

So stretch your arms way, way up
Take in a B-I-G breath of air.
Fill your W-H-O-L-E body up
With Warm Love and Good Care.

And when you let your breath out,
Place your hands on your heart.
Fill your whole being with light,
Relax any tight parts.

Look down and say "Thank You!"
"Dear Feet, you have carried me through."
"I feel so blessed and grateful,"
"For ALL that you do!"

Golden Sun has gone down now,

Silver Moon welcomes the night.

Feel that Starlight inside you

Burning brighter than bright!

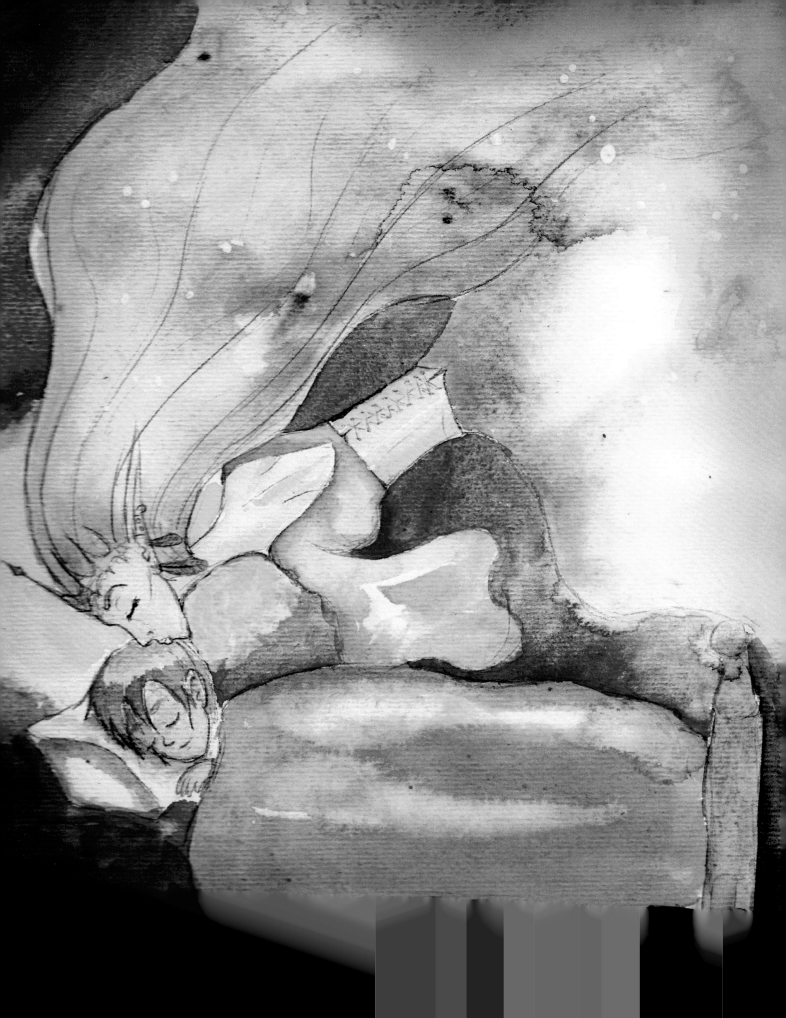

Night Night, Little Sweetheart,
Your day is complete.
The Sock Fairy Loves You,
From your head to your feet!

WHAT DO YOU THINK THE SOCK FAIRY LOOKS LIKE?

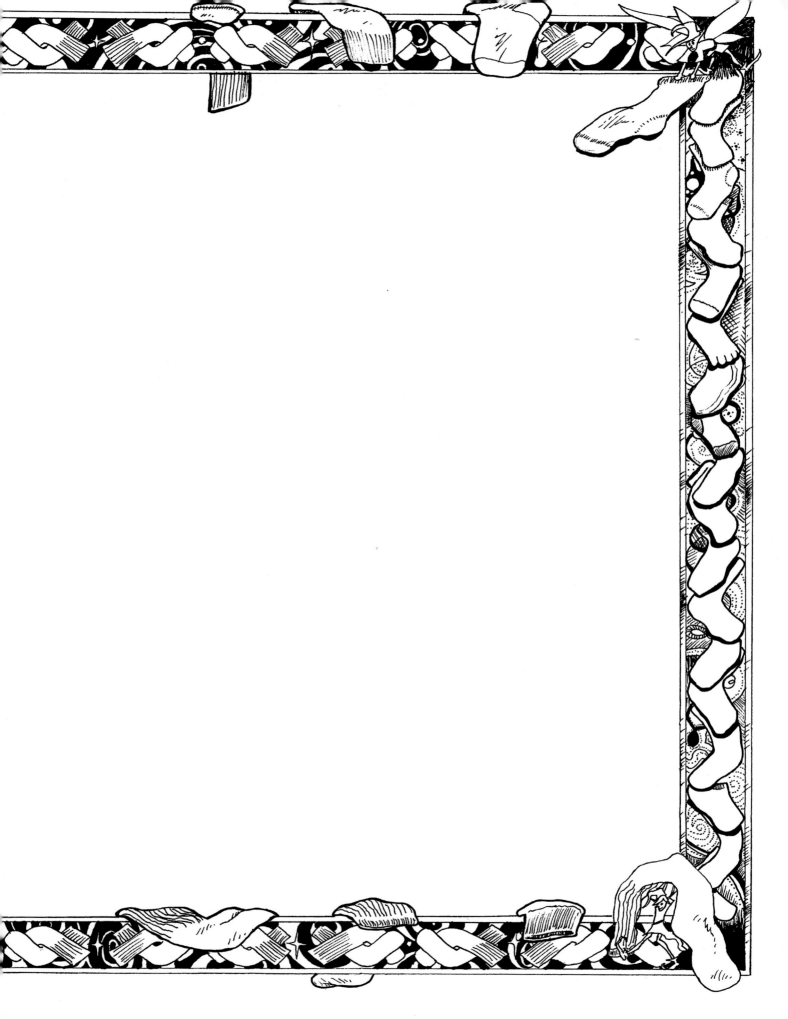